Pearl

THE FLYING UNICORN

SALLY ODGERS ILLUSTRATED BY ADELE K THOMAS

FEIWEL AND FRIENDS ♥ NEW YORK

For Imogen Grace —SALLY ODGERS

To Mum & Dad, for supplying my childhood
with endless art supplies and teaching me to
color within the lines —ADELE K THOMAS

A FEIWEL AND FRIENDS BOOK
An imprint of Macmillan Publishing Group, LLC
120 Broadway, New York, NY 10271

Our books may be purchased in bulk for promotional, educational, or business use.
Please contact your local bookseller or the Macmillan Corporate and
Premium Sales Department at (800) 221-7945 ext. 5442 or by email at
MacmillanSpecialMarkets@macmillan.com.

Library of Congress Control Number: 2019946633
ISBN 978-1-250-23552-7 (hardcover) / ISBN 978-1-250-23553-4 (ebook)

Feiwel and Friends logo designed by Filomena Tuosto

Originally published in 2018 in Australia by Scholastic Australia under the title
Pearl the Flying Unicorn.

First US edition, 2020

10 9 8 7 6 5 4 3 2 1

mackids.com

Chapter 1

It was a gusty, blustery day in the Kingdom, and Pearl the magical unicorn was off to meet her best friends, Olive and Tweet.

Olive was an ogre. She was stronger than anyone Pearl knew. If anything needed lifting, then Olive could do it. She also loved to eat. Pearl and Tweet were always surprised at how much ogres could eat without getting full.

Tweet the firebird was the smallest of the three friends. She could fly but she often preferred to ride on Olive's shoulder or cling to Pearl's mane. She was so small and light her friends sometimes forgot where she was perched.

On this gusty, blustery day, Olive and Tweet were waiting down by the pond for Pearl.

"**Leaping lions**, Olive!" said Pearl. "Is that a new hat?"

"Aunt Olga gave it to me," Olive said. "Isn't it wonderful?"

Olive's hat was made of yellow straw, and it was decorated with bright pink glitter feathers.

Tweet fluttered up to have a good look. "Pretty, like me!" she squawked. She looked at her own tail feathers and giggled.

HEE!
HEE!

"Now you both have feathers," Pearl said happily.

"Let's try it on you, Pearl," suggested Olive. She took off the hat and put it on Pearl's head. It was hard to make it sit properly. Pearl's horn got in the way.

"I don't think unicorns wear hats, Olive," Pearl said.

She leaned over the pond to look at her reflection. Then, suddenly, the hat fell off Pearl's head and the wind caught it!

Up, up, up it went in the air across the pond.

"Oh no!" Pearl said. She tried to use her magic to bring the hat back.

Flick-flick-flickety-flick!

"Watch out, Pearl!" yelled Olive, but it was too late. Pink sparkles fizzed in the air and sprinkled all over Olive's hat. The hat bounced upward and the feathers blew away in a sparkling cloud toward the sea.

Oops.

"I'm sorry, Olive," Pearl said.

"Never mind, you didn't mean it.
If we run up to the cliffs, we can
get them back," Olive said.

"Jump on!" said Pearl to her
friends. "Hurry, the feathers
are getting away!"

Olive jumped onto Pearl's back and
Tweet flew along.

Together, the three friends raced past the pond and up the path to the cliffs.

The glitter feathers whirled up in a cloud, then spun in circles.

Pearl bounded into the air while Olive held on with one hand and tried to grab the feathers with the other.

"Whee!" Tweet sang in delight.

She fluttered her wings and flew out from the cliff to help. The biggest glitter feather floated in the air. Excitedly, she grabbed for it with her talons.

"Got one! Look!" she said, tumbling over in a somersault.

WHEE!

Tweet's delight ended in a squawk of fear as the wind caught her and blew her out to sea.

"Flittering firebird!" cried Pearl. "Tweet! Come back here!"

"Can't!" squawked Tweet in a panic. Her wings flapped quickly against the wind.

"Hold on, Tweet!" cried Olive.

Pearl and Olive stared after their
friend. Tweet was in trouble. How were
they going to help her?

HELP!

Chapter 2

Olive reached out as far as she could with her ogre arms and tried to grab Tweet. But she was too far away. She couldn't reach her.

"Use your magic, Pearl," Olive urged.

Pearl wasn't sure. What if she made Tweet fly even farther away like she had done with the glitter feathers?

"Pearl!" Tweet called to her, wings flapping madly. "Help!"

Pearl thought quickly. Maybe she could make a net appear?

Flick–flick–swish! went Pearl.

Nothing happened.

Pearl tried again.

Flick-flickety-flick-prance-flick!

The wind bounced Tweet higher. Oh no!

Flick-flickety-flick-prance-flick-kick!
went Pearl. Then up Pearl went . . .
right into the air.

"**Bolting buckets!**" cried
Pearl as she floated away from the
cliff.

She was frightened.

She was floating.

She was FLYING!

Pearl kicked her feet and flew toward Tweet, who grabbed hold of Pearl's horn.

Olive leaned out from the cliff and grabbed the very end of Pearl's tail. She pulled as hard as she could, and soon Pearl and Tweet were back on the cliff, safe.

"Thanks!" spluttered Tweet. "Wind
got me!"

"It's all right now," said Olive. "You're
safe. And you saved one of my feathers!"
She stuck the feather in her pocket.
Then she stared in wonder at Pearl.
"Pearl, you flew!"

"Ooh, I did! I didn't know unicorns could fly!"

Olive laughed. "How could you know? You're the only unicorn in the Kingdom."

"You did it! You did!" Tweet said happily. "Do it again!"

"Ooh, yes!" Pearl was thrilled. She tossed her mane. She stamped her hoof.

"Fly, Pearl!" Tweet raised her wings and then lowered them quickly before the wind could take her again.

"I—I—I don't quite remember how," said Pearl. She thought hard. "Um, did you see what I did?"

"Bit busy blowing away," said Tweet.

"Bit busy grabbing for Tweet," Olive said. "I know there were flicks and a prance."

Flickety-prance-flick! went Pearl.

A small pink cupcake fell from the sky and landed on Olive's head.

"Yum!" said Olive, grabbing the cupcake and biting it in half with her ogre teeth. "Delicious!"

Pearl flicked and pranced, kicked and
flicked, but she couldn't manage to fly.

"Sorry, Olive. I don't think I'll be able
to fly after your feathers."

"Well, you saved Tweet, and that's more important than any feathers," Olive said. She hugged Pearl.

Together, they watched as the feathers blew out to sea. "I wonder where they'll land," Olive added.

"Floating flamingos," Pearl said gloomily. "I wish we could have caught them."

Suddenly the gusty, blustery wind stopped. Pearl sighed with relief. She liked the wind, but it wasn't safe for Tweet.

"Ooh, look!" Olive said, leaning over the edge of the cliff. "The glitter feathers are coming down over there on Gull Island. I'll get my ogre boat. We can row to the island!"

Chapter 3

The three friends walked down to the harbor where Olive kept her ogre boat. Olive used her ogre strength to push the boat into the water.

"Let's go," she said.

Tweet perched on the bow and Olive got in the paddling seat.

"Come on, Pearl."

"I don't think I'll fit, Olive," Pearl pointed out. "I'm too big."

"Try," said Tweet.

Pearl tried to get into the ogre boat.
She got her front hooves in, but there
was nowhere to put
her back ones.

She tried
sitting in tail-
first, but her
legs hung over
the edge.

Olive and Tweet got out and Pearl got in. That worked, but there was no space for Olive to paddle.

"**Blundering bats.**" Pearl sulked. "I not only can't fly to get you to the island, but I can't come with you at all."

"Don't worry," Olive said. "You can watch us from the top of the cliff. Maybe you'll remember how to fly if you practice."

Olive and Tweet paddled away from the harbor, and Pearl trotted all the way back to the top of the cliff.

She looked down at Gull Island. The sand was covered with glitter feathers. They were so sparkly. No wonder Olive wanted to get them back.

Pearl stamped her hoof. She wanted to be with her friends. What was the point of being a magical unicorn if she had to be stuck on a cliff top?

She was going to keep practicing.

"Let's see, maybe it was flick-flickety-flick-prance-kick-kick!" She tried that.

Pink sparkles zinged into the air. Then a passing seagull cried out in surprise as it turned bright pink. "Ooh, look at me! I'm bea-YOO-ti-ffull," the seagull said before flying away.

AWWWK!

Maybe I have to jump into the air? thought Pearl. She flicked her tail three times, then added a prance and a wiggle and a kick.

Nothing happened.

Pearl sighed. **Purple parsnips! Maybe I need some wind to get off the ground?**

She looked down over the wide blue bay. It was so calm and gentle now that the wind had blown itself away. Olive's ogre boat looked like a toy from up high. Olive and Tweet were singing as they paddled along.

"Row, row your ogre boat
Gently in the sea,
Ogrely, ogrely, ogrely, ogrely
Lots of snacks for me."

"**Cackling cakes**, why am I so big?" Pearl moped. "Olive and Tweet are having so much fun in the ogre boat."

But Olive and Tweet weren't the only ones having fun in the bay. As Pearl looked out to sea, another boat appeared. It was heading for Gull Island, too.

Maybe it's another ogre boat? thought Pearl. "It's probably another ogre and another firebird and someone like me, only smaller, so she can fit in the ogre boat."

Pearl squinted into the sunlight as the other boat came closer. But it didn't look like an ogre boat. Ogre boats were round. They bobbed cheerfully along, because ogres liked to bop around as they rowed.

HMMM

This boat wasn't round.

This boat wasn't bobbing and bopping.

This boat was sneaking and snaking.

This boat was moving in a grouchy, mean jitter.

Instead of having cheerful pink paint, this boat was an ugly shade of brown like old squashed bananas. It had a flag flying from a pole. Pearl couldn't quite see what the picture was, but she knew she didn't like it.

Then a cold shiver went through her as
she realized it wasn't an ogre boat at all.

It was a gobble-un boat.

It was rowed by three gobble-uns. And they weren't just any old gobble-uns.

They were gobble-un pirates!

"Slippery salad!" cried Pearl. "They're heading straight for Olive and Tweet!"

Chapter 4

Olive!" yelled Pearl, prancing around worriedly on top of the cliff. "Olive, look behind you!"

Olive must have seen her prancing, because she let go of the paddle and waved cheerfully.

Tweet flapped her wings and waved, too.

"Olive! Tweet! Behind you!" cried Pearl again, but the wind picked up and snatched her words away.

Olive and Tweet started to sing again.

"Row, row your ogre boat
Gently in the sun,
Ogrely, ogrely, ogrely, ogrely
Pears and peas are yum."

Pearl stamped her hoof. Her friends couldn't hear her because of the wind.

The gobble-un boat was getting closer, and now Pearl could see the picture on the flag. It was made from bones!

If only she were closer. Then Pearl had an idea. She knew what she needed to do.

Flick-flickety-flick-prance-flick-kick!

Pearl closed her eyes and jumped right off the cliff.

Out she sailed, tail tossing, mane swishing. She was doing it! She was floating! She was flying! She knew she could do it!

"Awwwk!" A group of seagulls swooped toward her.

"Pearl! Pearl! We want to be pink!"

PINK!

PEARL!

"Boiled buttons, not now!" yelled Pearl.

"Pink, too!" The gulls kept swooping. "We want to be bea-YOO-ti-ffull!"

Pearl tried to dodge them, but she lost her concentration and fell, tumbling in the air,

DOWN,

DOWN,

DOWN . . .

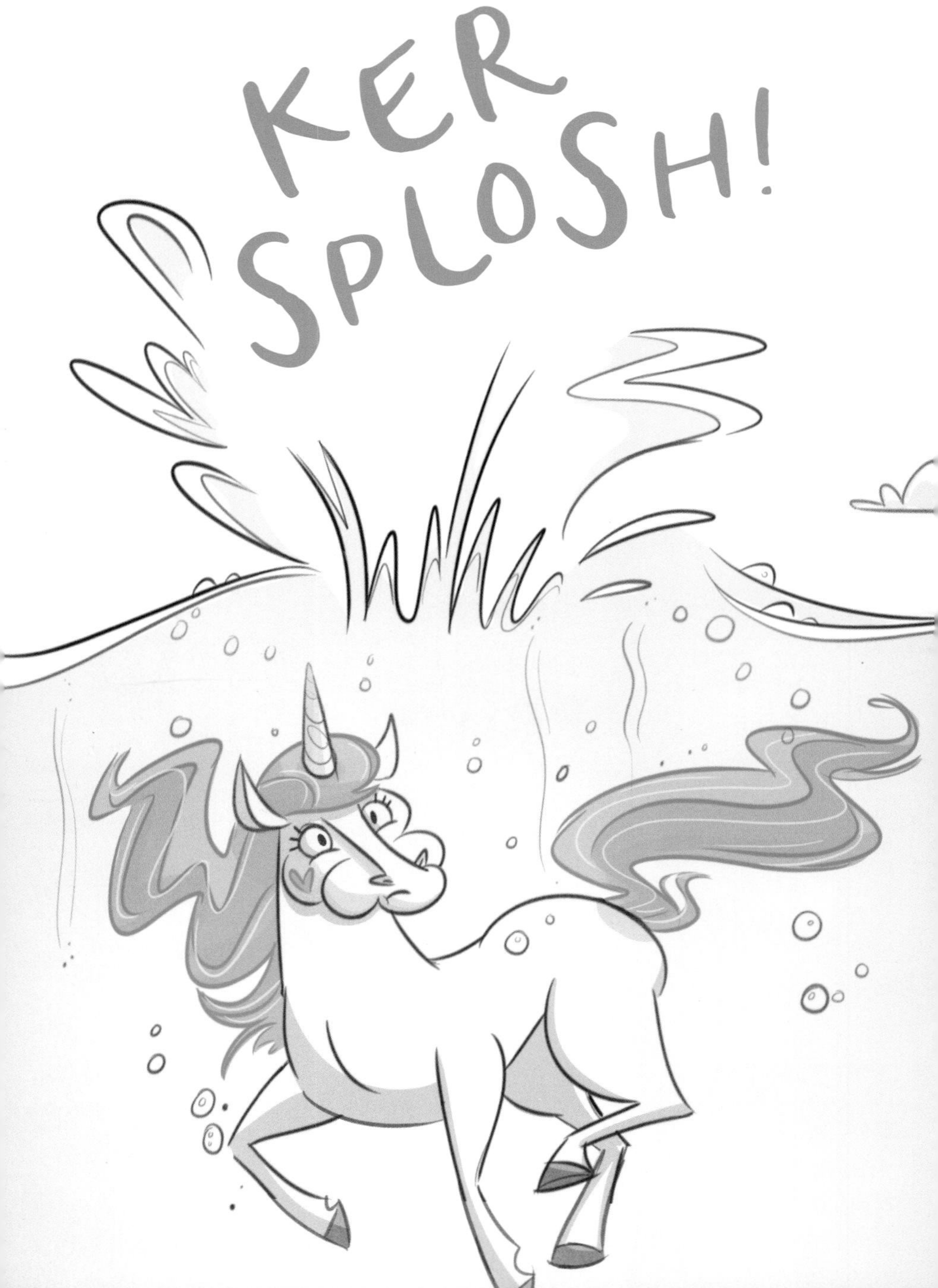
KER
SPLOSH!

Pearl was now swimming in the sea,
much too close to the gobble-un
pirate boat.

Ugh. The squashed
banana color was even
worse close up.

Chapter 5

The gobble-un pirates had been rowing after the ogre boat, but when Pearl landed in the water, they stopped chasing Olive and Tweet.

When they saw Pearl, the biggest gobble-un's eyes lit up with nasty glee.

"Unicorn stew!" it yelled. "Come on, me nasties!"

The whole boat started singing.

"Sixteen bugs on a gobble-un's hat! Stinky, pinky, yuckety splat! Stinky, pinky, yuckety spew! Now we're gonna have unicorn stew!"

The gobble-un pirate boat turned around and set off toward Pearl.

"No!" yelled the medium-size gobble-un. "Glitter feathers first, and make 'em stinky. Unicorn stew later."

"Stew now!" yelled the biggest gobble-un, twitching its fingers.

"Feathers! Yuckety stink!" yelled the medium gobble-un. It used an oar and bopped the biggest gobble-un on the head.

BOP!

The biggest gobble-un then pushed
the medium gobble-un, jumped up,
and waved a fist at Pearl. "We're
gonna get you, unicorn!"

"Yuckety spew! Unicorn STEW!"
howled the pirates.

All this noise was horrible to hear, but there was one good thing about it. The noise made Olive and Tweet look behind them.

"Pirates!" screamed Pearl, splashing around. She paddled hard with all her hooves.

"Row, row, row away as fast as you can!" Pearl spluttered.

But Olive didn't. Olive let out a big ogre yell. "You're not going to stew our Pearl!" Then she started paddling straight for the gobble-un pirate boat!

"CHARRRGE!"

Olive and Tweet
raced along
the water.

"**Clomping cats!** Olive, NO!" cried Pearl. "Go the other way! I can swim back!"

She was too late. The boat of gobble-uns had turned to see what all the yelling was about. They forgot about Pearl and rowed straight for Olive's ogre boat.

They were going to CRASH!

Pearl kicked wildly in the water. Then
her back hoof struck something hard.

It was a rock. A rock in the water!
Pearl stood on top of it. Yes! There was
no time to waste. She had to use her
magic.

Flick-flickety-kick-splosh-nod-FLICK!
went Pearl. She wasn't sure what
that one did, but she hoped it was
something good.

A cloud of pink butterflies whooshed into the air and fluttered toward the gobble-uns' boat. They flickered and flittered, trailing their silky pink wings right over the gobble-uns' heads.

The gobble-uns stopped rowing.

"Pink butterflies! Flutterfies!
Bufferplies! Pink!" they howled,
jumping and weaving to get away
from the pretty things.

The gobble-un pirate boat rocked wildly from side to side.

Then the biggest gobble-un fell into the water with a SPLASH!

The other two gobble-uns pointed and laughed.

"Pull me out, you horrible hoppers," yelled the biggest gobble-un. He spat out a mouthful of water.

The medium gobble-un stuck out an oar and pulled the biggest one up to safety.

Dripping, the biggest gobble-un crawled into the boat. "Pink flufferfies!" he cried. "Don't let 'em get me."

"They're gone," said the medium gobble-un. "The splash scared 'em all away."

"Yuck, you're clean," said the smallest one, staring.

"No clean gobble-uns in the pirate boat," roared the medium-size gobble-un. "Gobble-un pirates are never clean. You go and get filthy."

They pushed the biggest gobble-un
back into the water.

While the gobble-uns were arguing,
Pearl swam over to Olive's ogre boat.
"Olive, what are you doing? Why were
you chasing the gobble-un pirates?"
asked Pearl.

"Stew song!"
squawked Tweet.

"We couldn't let them do anything horrible to you," Olive explained.

"**Paddling pears**, Olive, they couldn't stew me. They haven't got a stew pot! You were the ones in trouble."

"Oh." Olive blushed. "I never thought of that."

"Pink flutters!" shrieked Tweet. "Wheeeee! SPLOSH!" She flapped her wings.

Olive and Tweet hugged Pearl.

"You were so clever to send the pink
butterflies to scare the gobble-un
pirates," Olive said.

Pearl didn't tell her friends that she'd
done it by accident.

"Let's go get those feathers!" said Olive.

Chapter 6

By the time Pearl reached Gull Island, Olive and Tweet were already gathering the glitter feathers.

Olive picked them up and crammed them into her pockets.

"Look!" Olive said. "These are the ones that blew off my hat, but there are lots more, too."

Tweet jumped straight into a pile and kicked her feet in the air.

Pearl was tired, and dripping with water, but she loved seeing her friends having so much fun.

Olive emptied her feathers into the ogre boat. "I have plenty to make a new hat, but if we collect more, Tweet can have some to make a little coat for special occasions."

"Some for Pearl, too!" squawked Tweet.

"We could make a unicorn hat with a hole for your horn," Olive said.

Pearl smiled. She didn't need a hat, but if her friends wanted her to have one, she'd wear it.

"We'd better go before those gobble-un pirates come back," Pearl said.

Olive pushed the ogre boat back into the water.

"Pearl, are you ready to swim back?" asked Olive.

"I think I'll try flying again," Pearl said.

Olive and Tweet paddled away as Pearl took a big breath. Soon she'd be flying over the sea. She'd circle up over the cliffs and surprise the seagulls.

Flickety-flick-prance-kick-kick!

She leaped into the air . . .

Up, up, and . . .

PLONK.

Pearl hit the sand. She got up and tried again.

Flickety-flick-prance-kick-kick!

Pearl sprang into the air once more.

Up, up, and . . .

Pearl stamped her hoof. **"Tossing tadpoles!** Why can't I do it? The wind's blowing nicely. Maybe I need a run-up."

Just then, Pearl heard something horrible.

It was a gobble-un song!

The biggest gobble-un was back in the pirate boat, and all three pirates were rowing hard toward the ogre boat.

"Sixteen bugs on
a gobble-un's hat!
Stinky, pinky, yuckety splat!
Stinky, pinky, yuckety spew!
Now we're gonna have ogre stew!
Stinky, pinky, filthy pew!
And we're gonna stew firebird, too."

"And pick our teeth with the
feathers!" yelled the smallest gobble-un.

Pearl tossed her mane. She had to
rescue Olive and Tweet!

Chapter 7

Flick-flickety-flick-prance-flick-kick!
Pearl thought of her best friends and
leaped high into the air. She closed her
eyes and pretended she was galloping
across a green meadow and up a hill.

This time there was no plonk of hooves.
Instead she felt lighter than air.

Pearl opened her eyes.

She was doing it! She was flying!
Below her was the blue bay. Pearl
took a deep breath to call out to her
friends but then decided not to in case
she lost her concentration and fell
into the sea again.

The pirate gobble-uns were still rowing after Olive's ogre boat and they were getting closer and closer!

Pearl flew over the pirate boat, but although the pirates stopped singing their stew song, they didn't stop rowing.

What to do? thought Pearl.

Oh, if only she could knock those
pirates back into the sea! All of them!
If only she could make the ogre boat fly
. . . Wait! Maybe she could!

Flick-flickety-flick-prance-flick-kick!
went Pearl in the air.

Pink sparks flew, hitting the ogre boat and making it sparkle.

Pearl concentrated hard on lifting the ogre boat.

"Hold on!" cried Pearl.

Then Olive looked up. "Pearl! You can do it."

"You can do it!" squawked Tweet. "Wheeeee!"

Olive clung to the ogre boat, and Tweet clung to Olive.

Jumping jelly beans! It was working!

Up came the ogre boat, swinging over the top of the pirate gobble-uns.

"Hee-hee!" laughed Tweet, shaking her tail at them.

The biggest one roared as he reached up to grab the ogre boat. Olive lifted her paddle and bopped him on the nose.

BOP!

The biggest gobble-un yelled and
shook his fist.

"I'll stew you for this, unicorn!"

"Stop 'em! They're getting away!"
howled the other gobble-uns.

Flying herself and the ogre boat was the hardest thing Pearl had ever done in her life, but she wasn't going to give up now. And thank goodness the harbor was right underneath her.

"Hang on!" she called down to her friends.

Pearl landed with a thud of hooves, and the ogre boat splashed down in the harbor. Olive jumped ashore and dragged the boat onto the sand.

Pearl's friends were safely on shore, but the pirate gobble-uns were still rowing. They could still catch Olive and Tweet.

Suddenly Pearl had a great idea. Gobble-uns hated pink. They also hated being clean, so . . .

Kickety-kick-kick-flick! went Pearl.

Pink sparkles shot out over the gobble-un pirate boat.

For a moment, it seemed as if nothing would happen. Then . . .

SPLOOOSH!

A shower of pink soapsuds covered the gobble-uns and their boat.

The gobble-un pirates howled in fright.

"Ugh! Yuck! Pink! We're clean!"

"Quick, quick, stinky magic!"

"Argh! The boat's sinking!"

The dirt that had held the boat
together had started to dissolve
in the thick pink soap.

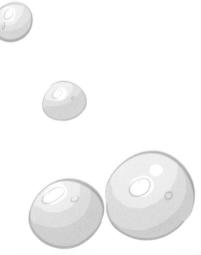

On the shore, Olive and Tweet stood
staring at the sight of three clean,
soapy pirate gobble-uns leaping out
of their sinking boat. Splashing and
howling, the gobble-uns swam away.

Tweet pointed with her wing and
started to giggle. Before long, she was
kicking her feet and squawking
loudly with laughter.

Pearl laughed, too. She was so happy
that she could help her friends.

Olive turned to Pearl and grinned her
big ogre grin. "I knew you could do it,
Pearl. You're the best unicorn friend
an ogre and a firebird could have."

"It felt so good to fly," Pearl said. "You know my magic often goes wrong."

"I know," said Olive, "but when it matters . . . when it really, really matters . . . then it goes right." She sighed. "All that rowing's made me hungry."

"I'll magic up some marshmallows!" said Pearl happily.

Flick-kick-flick!

Out flew pink sparks.

Down came . . . a pile of cucumbers and strawberries.

"Oops!" said Pearl.

"Yum! My favorite!" said Olive. As she ate the strawberries, she started collecting the glitter feathers they had found.

CRUNCH!

Tweet leaped feetfirst into the pile of
strawberries and buried her beak in
the biggest one. "Yum!"

"Oops," said Olive as one of
her glitter feathers flew
up into the air.

"I'll get it!" Tweet flapped her wings and flew up. "Wheeeee! Got it!" Her glee ended in a startled squawk as the wind got serious, taking the firebird and blowing her up and over the sea again.

"Help!" cried Tweet.

Pearl sighed. "Jump on, Olive," she said.
"I'll fly, you catch, and please don't lose
your feathers!"

DON'T MISS PEARL'S FIRST MAGICAL ADVENTURE!

SALLY ODGERS was born in Tasmania, Australia, in 1957, and has lived there ever since. Sally began writing as a child, and her first book was published in 1977. More than 250 books have followed, including *Good Night, Truck.* She is married to Darrel Odgers, and they have two adult children, James and Tegan. Darrel and Sally live in a house full of books, music, and Jack Russell terriers.

SALLYODGERS.WEEBLY.COM

ADELE K THOMAS is a Melbourne-based illustrator, director, and art director with over ten years of design experience in animation production, TV, children's books, advertising, and apps.

ADELEKTHOMAS.COM

Thank you for reading this
Feiwel and Friends book.
The friends who made

THE FLYING UNICORN

possible are

Jean Feiwel, Publisher

Liz Szabla, Associate Publisher

Rich Deas, Senior Creative Director

Holly West, Senior Editor

Anna Roberto, Senior Editor

Kat Brzozowski, Senior Editor

Alexei Esikoff, Senior Managing Editor

Kim Waymer, Senior Production Manager

Erin Siu, Assistant Editor

Emily Settle, Associate Editor

Foyinsi Adegbonmire, Editorial Assistant

Sophie Erb, Associate Designer

Lindsay Wagner, Production Editor

Follow us on Facebook or visit us online at mackids.com.
Our books are friends for life!